THE CAT IN THE CAGE
and other GREAT STORIES for kids

JERRY D. THOMAS

Pacific Press® Publishing Association
Nampa, Idaho
Oshawa, Ontario, Canada

Editor: Aileen Andres Sox
Designer: Robert N. Mason
Cover Layout: Michelle Petz
Illustration/Art Direction: Justinen Creative Group
Typeset in Century Old Style 13/17

ISBN 0-8163-1420-9

04 05 06 07 08 • 10 9 8 7

Contents

Feathers and Puzzle

1

Bye, Elena. See you tomorrow."

Elena turned to wave at her friends from school and then walked on alone down her block. She pulled on the straps to her backpack and mumbled to herself.

"My books sure are heavy today. All because of Mrs. Carmichael. I'll never finish all my science homework."

Elena fished for the shoestring looped around her neck under her sweater. She pulled it out and grabbed the shiny key as she walked up to the next-to-the-last gray stone building on Gulliver Street. Her key fit perfectly in the door to Apartment 117.

"Puzzle," she called as she opened the door. "I'm home, Puzzle." As always, Elena pushed the door shut behind her. Then she locked the

Latchkey kids; handling emergencies

Feathers and Puzzle

doorknob, turned the deadbolt lock, and slipped the golden chain into place.

Before she finished, Puzzle was rubbing her legs and crying for attention. "Hello, Puzzle," Elena said, scratching behind her cat's ear just the way he liked it.

Meow, purrr-purrr. Puzzle rolled over on the black-and-orange spots that gave him his name. He wanted his belly scratched. But Elena patted him once and walked away.

"Feathers, I'm home," she called. But Feathers already knew. She was fluttering and chirping in her cage. *Chir-reep!*

"Hi, Feathers." Elena opened the bird-cage door and reached in. Feathers hopped onto her finger and chirped again. "Time for food and water. Let's go get some."

Elena moved her finger closer to her chest, and the lovebird fluttered over to her shoulder. "Sorry I don't have a pocket to put you in today. That always has been your favorite place to hide." Elena laughed. She grabbed the food and water

dishes from their places on the cage wires and walked to the kitchen sink. Puzzle padded along behind.

"No, Puzzle, I'm not forgetting you. I'll get your food next."

Elena talked to her pets a lot. They kept her company in the apartment until her mom got home from work. Elena was used to being there with only her pets, but her mom still worried.

"Remember," her mom had said that morning, as she did every morning, "lock the door behind you, and don't open it for anyone."

"Yes, Mother."

"And what do you tell people who call on the phone?"

"My mother can't come to the phone right now. May I take a message?" Elena knew it all by heart.

"And if there is an emergency?"

"Call 9-1-1 for help."

Elena carefully balanced the seed and water containers and walked back to the living room. Feathers fluttered and stuck her head up as Elena reached into the bird cage.

Chir-reep! Feathers said.

"I know," Elena said with a frown. "I need to change the paper in the bottom of your cage. Mom said I had to do it before she gets home." She wrinkled her nose at the dirty job. "I'll do it later."

After eating an orange, watching a couple of cartoon shows, and doing a few minutes of homework, Elena knew she couldn't put it off any longer. "All right, Feathers, let's clean up." Lifting the bird cage off its stand, she set it on the table and unhooked the bottom from the wire sides.

"You wait here," Elena said as she set the top part of the cage on the table. Feathers didn't seem to mind. Then Elena carried the dirty newspaper-covered bottom to the trash can.

"This is gross," she muttered as she dumped it in.

Crash! The loud sound made Elena jump and drop the cage bottom.

"Aaaah!" She was screaming before it even hit the floor. *Someone is trying to break in!* she thought for a second. But not for

much longer.

Before she could even blink, a flurry of feathers and fur rushed past her. Without even looking, Elena knew what had happened. Puzzle had knocked Feathers's cage off the table. And now he was after her!

"Puzzle, stop!" The cat followed the bird into the kitchen

Feathers and Puzzle

without even slowing down. Elena joined the chase. "Feathers, come here!" Feathers fluttered to a stop on the counter by the sink. But before Elena could get there, Puzzle leapt up toward the bird.

Cheep! Feathers escaped from Puzzle's paws by a feather and headed back out into the living room.

Meow! Puzzle escaped from Elena's hands by a hair and leapt after the bird.

"No!" Elena cried. "Puzzle, come back here!"

Feathers skipped from the table to the back of the couch. Puzzle did the same. Feathers flew to the television, then up to the curtain rod over the window. Puzzle was just one step behind. From the TV, he leapt halfway up the curtain and started climbing, one paw at a time.

"No!"

At that same second, the nails holding the curtain rod pulled out of the wall. Curtain rod, curtain, cat, and bird all fell to the floor.

Elena forgot to scream. For a second, she just stared. Nothing moved under the curtain. "Oh no," she whispered. "Feathers, are you OK?" she almost shouted as she ran to the jumbled pile on the floor.

"Feathers, where are you?" Elena pawed through the curtains until she saw green feathers. "Oh no." Elena picked up her bird. Feathers was still.

"Nothing looks broken." Elena lifted Feathers's wings. Then she got mad. "Puzzle, you are a bad cat. I'm going to . . . Puzzle?"

There, under the curtain rod, was Puzzle. And he wasn't moving, either.

"Oh no! They're both dead!"

Emergency!

2

N o, no, no," Elena mumbled under her breath as she lifted Feathers's still body up to look at it more closely. "You can't be dead." Then she saw it. The bird's green chest was moving. She was breathing!

"She's alive." Elena lay the bird carefully on the couch and went back to her cat. Kneeling down beside the curtains, she looked carefully at him. He was breathing too!

Elena shook him gently. "Puzzle, wake up!" But the cat just lay there—breathing but not moving.

"What should I do?" Elena asked herself, trying not to cry. "I'm afraid they're both going to die." She tried to think. "I'll call Mom at work." Then she looked at the clock. "I can't call Mom—she's already on her way home."

She paced back to the couch. "I have to do something. This is an emergency!"

Suddenly, Elena knew what to do. She picked up the phone and punched three buttons: 9-1-1.

Latchkey kids; handling emergencies

"Emergency Services," a woman's voice said. "What is the problem?"

"This is an emergency," Elena said with a trembling voice. "I'm afraid they're going to die."

"OK, sweetheart," the operator said, "take it easy. Can you tell me your name and your address?"

"My name is Elena. I live at 1458 Gulliver Street, Apartment 117," Elena recited.

"Elena, are any adults with you?"

"No. My mom isn't home from work yet." Elena could hear the operator talking to other people for a moment. Then she was back.

"OK, Elena. An ambulance is on its way. Luckily, a police car was near your street, so it will be there very soon. Now, tell me what happened."

Elena was so worried and afraid she couldn't think very well. She tried to explain. "I don't know why he did it. He's never tried to hurt her before! They've lived here together for a long time."

"What happened? How is she injured?"

"She took off to get away from him. Then the curtain fell. I think the curtain rod hit him on the head." As she spoke, Elena saw something move in the living room. "Wait, he's moving! He's shaking his head! I think he's OK!"

"Who?"

"Puzzle. He was chasing Feathers."

There was silence for a second. Through the window, Elena could see the lights of the police car coming down her street. Somehow, even before the operator said another word, Elena knew she was in trouble.

"Are we talking about your pets?"

Elena wanted to slam down the phone and hide under the table. But it was too late for that. The police car was stopping in front of her house. "Yes," she said quietly. "My bird and my cat. Puzzle was chasing Feathers, and they both got hurt."

"Elena, 9-1-1 is for people emergencies, not animals." Over the phone, Elena could hear the operator talking to someone else. "There is no emergency. Call the ambulance back."

The lights on the police car out on the street snapped off. Elena's voice quivered. "But what about Feathers and Puzzle?"

"Since the officers are already there, they'll come check on you. I'll stay on the phone until they get to your door."

Ding-dong. "That's the officers now. You can open the door."

Elena wasn't so sure. "My mom told me not to open the door for anyone when she's not home."

"And she's exactly right," the woman said, "but we know these are police officers, so it's OK."

Elena hung up and looked through the peephole. Then she turned the locks, unhooked the chain, and opened the door.

"Are you Elena?" one of the two officers asked. She nodded. "I'm Officer Carter, and this is Officer Martinez. Elena, you know you're not supposed to call 9-1-1 unless it's really an emergency, don't you?"

Elena nodded. A tear trickled down her cheek. "She told me that on the phone; 9-1-1 is only for people emergencies. But Mr. Carter, this is an animal emergency. My bird is hurt."

Officer Carter nodded toward his partner. "I'll go have a look. Shout if something comes up." Officer Martinez nodded and headed back to the car. Officer Carter followed Elena inside.

By now, Puzzle was sitting up, licking his paws. "Feathers

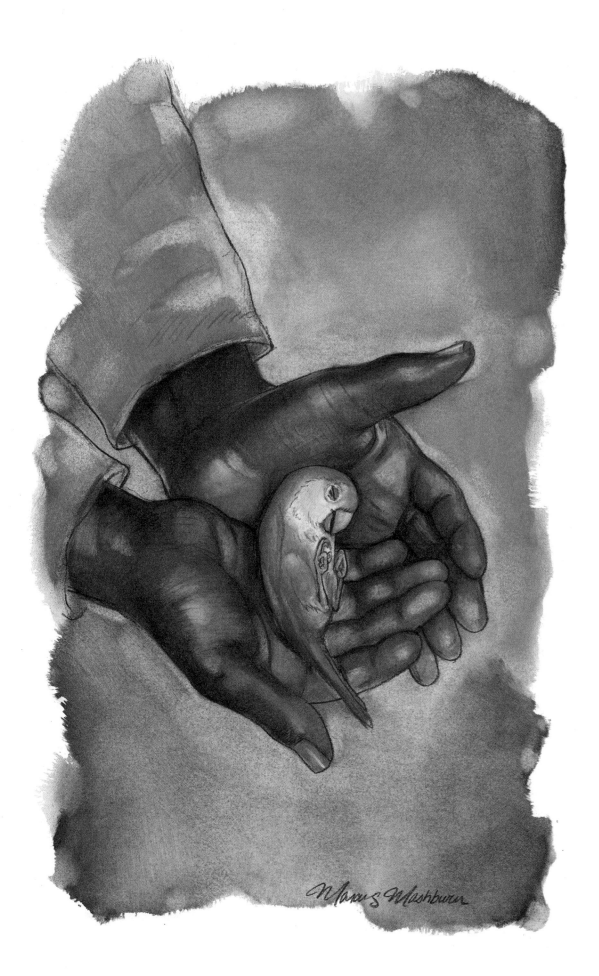

is over here on the couch," Elena said.

Officer Carter picked up the little lump of green feathers. "She's still breathing. Elena, your bird is probably in shock. That means she got too scared. If you wrap her up in a towel to keep her warm and talk to her, she should be OK."

"I'll hold her in my hand close to my chest," Elena decided. "I wish I had a pocket."

Just then, Elena heard a voice outside by the street. "What's going on? Officer, is my baby OK?"

"Oops," Elena mumbled. "I forgot about . . ."

Emergency!

But the door crashed open before she could finish. "Elena, are you all right?"

"Sure, Mom. I'm fine." Elena tried to answer while her mother hugged her tight. "But Feathers is in shock."

"That makes two of us," Mom said, pushing Elena back at arm's length. "What are the police doing here?"

Elena tried to explain. "I was cleaning the cage like you told me, and Puzzle knocked it over, and Feathers flew, and I chased them, and the curtains fell on them, and, and . . ." Elena burst into tears and threw her arms around her mom's neck.

Cheep! The sound made Elena jump back. "Oh, Feathers! You're OK!" she said as looked into her hand.

Mom followed Officer Carter to the door. "Thank you so much. I'll make sure she understands."

Elena heard the locks click into place as she held Feathers up to her cheek. She knew what was coming next.

"Elena, we need to have a talk."

"Yes, Mom."

By the time she went to bed, Elena knew it by heart.

"Call 9-1-1 if you are hurt or in danger. Call 9-1-1 if you know another person is hurt or in danger. Otherwise, leave the police and the ambulances alone so they can help other people."

"This was all your fault," Elena whispered to Puzzle when he hopped up beside her pillow. "You deserved getting hit on the head."

Purrr-purrr. Puzzle closed his eyes and started his motor.

"Oh, well, I forgive you." Elena closed her eyes too.

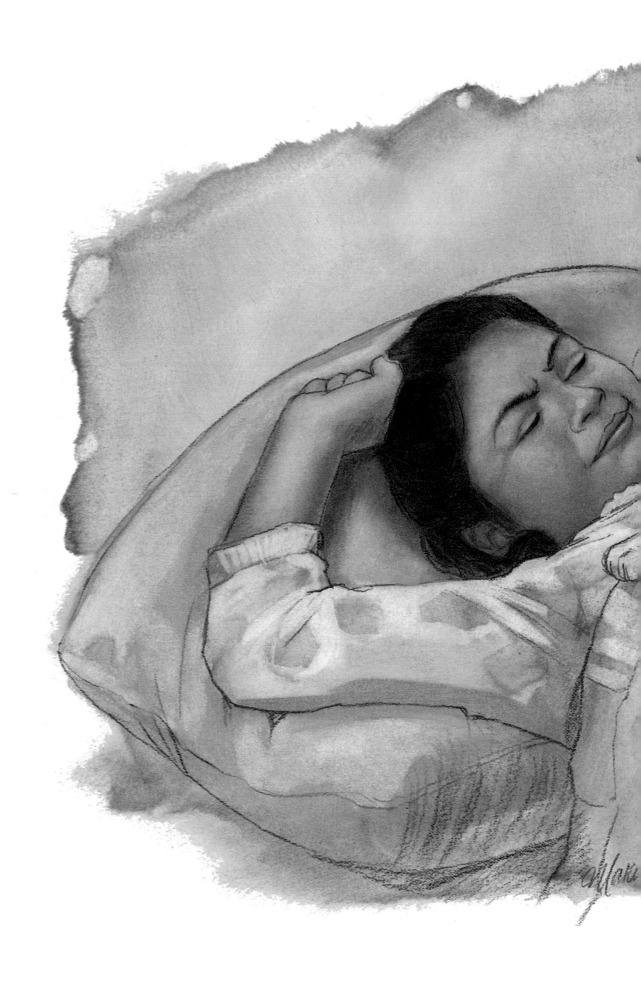

Smoke!

One afternoon several weeks later, the key turned in the lock again. "Puzzle, I'm home." *Click, clunk, clack.* Elena locked the door behind her.

Meow, purrr-purrr. Puzzle came crying for attention. "Hello, boy," Elena said, stopping to scratch his belly. "Feathers, I'm home," she called.

Chir-reep! Feathers answered.

Elena fed her pets and herself and then sat down to watch TV. "Puzzle," she asked a few minutes later, "is something wrong?"

The cat was prowling around the room, sniffing at the windows and the door. *Meow?* He seemed to be asking a question.

Before long, Elena noticed it too. "What is that smell? Is something burning?" She looked around but didn't see any smoke. Then, from far away, she heard the sound of a siren.

"Do you think it's a firetruck?" she asked Puzzle. They

Latchkey kids; handling emergencies

both stared out the window and listened. "I think it's getting closer."

By the time the firetruck turned down Gulliver Street, Elena was pacing back and forth like Puzzle. "I wonder how close the fire is? I could go outside and look, but Mom told

me not to open the door for any reason."

The smell of smoke got stronger. As Elena watched, more cars and trucks with flashing lights on top turned down her street. When she saw smoke moving like a cloud across the street, she picked up the phone.

"Mom's phone is busy," she reported to Puzzle. Suddenly,

she felt scared. "What am I supposed to do? Should I call 9-1-1?"

Chir-reep! Cheep! Feathers had something to say.

"I know, Feathers. When I called 9-1-1, I got in trouble. But Mom said to call if I am in danger. Do you think I am?"

Neither the bird nor the cat had an answer for that. Another cloud of smoke drifting by her window helped Elena decide. She picked up the phone again and punched three buttons.

"Emergency Services," a woman's voice said.

Elena took a deep breath. "My name is Elena, and I'm not sure if this is an emergency. But there are firetrucks in front of my apartment. Is my building on fire? What should I do?"

"What's your address, Elena?"

"1458 Gulliver Street, Apartment 117."

"OK, let me find out. Stay with me." Elena could hear the woman asking questions and talking to other people. Then she came back on. "Elena, the fire is in the building next to yours. But you need to leave in case it spreads. Is an adult with you?"

"No, just my cat and my bird. And my mom told me not to open the door or leave the apartment until she gets home."

"Elena, your mother wants you to be safe. Can you see a police car from your window?"

Elena peeked out. "Yes."

"I want you to open your door, close it behind you, and walk straight to that police car. Tell an officer where you live and that you're alone. Someone will watch you until your mother can get there. Will you do that?"

"OK," Elena agreed. She set down the phone and walked toward the door.

Chir-reep!

"Feathers! I can't leave you." She ran and grabbed the bird's cage off its hook.

Meow?

"Puzzle! Come here." Elena set the cage down and gathered her cat up in her arms. "What am I going to do with you? If I try to carry you outside, you'll get down and run away. But I can't leave you here. I wish you could fit in my pocket like a bird."

That gave her an idea. A few seconds later, she was ready.

Smoke swirled in as Elena opened her door. Coughing, she set down the bird cage and pulled the door closed behind her. She could hear the crackling roar of the fire and the wailing of another firetruck, but she couldn't see through the smoke.

Elena's hand shook as she picked up the bird cage. *Don't be scared,* she told herself. *Everything will be OK if I can see enough to get away without running into something.* With one hand shielding her eyes, Elena headed down her steps.

Bonk! She ran right into something.

"Aaah!" Elena screamed. The bird cage slipped out of her hand and hit the step.

"Whoa!" A police officer grabbed the cage with one hand and Elena's arm with the other. "I've got you. Are you the girl who called 9-1-1?"

Elena just coughed and nodded.

"Good. I was just coming to make sure you got out." He smiled at the bird cage. "I see you got your pet out. There's no one else at your house, right?"

"Right."

"OK, let's go." As they crossed the street, Elena watched the flames shooting from the roof and windows of the building next to hers. The firefighters were spraying water on it from three different trucks.

The officer led the way out of the smoke and over to a

crowd of people standing behind a yellow ribbon. "Officer Carter," he shouted, "here's another one to keep an eye on."

Officer Carter came right over. He stared for a second and then remembered her. "Oh, it's you, our 9-1-1 caller."

Elena smiled. "I called again today, and they told me to come out here. So I did."

"Well, it looks like you did exactly the right thing this time. Come on over to the police car, and we'll try to get in touch with your mother."

After hearing that her mom was on her way home, Elena stood and watched the fire with the other people. Slowly, the water was beating the flames down.

Officer Carter stopped to report. "It looks as if your home is safe, Elena." He patted the bird cage. "I hope your other pet is OK."

"Oh, Feathers is fine," Elena answered, patting her pocket. "But Puzzle will be mad at me for a week. Won't you?" she added, kneeling down to scratch her cat's head.

Meow! Puzzle grumped from behind the bars of the bird cage.

Happy to Be Arrested!

4

Do you like this one?" Evie held up the shirt for her friends to see.

Candace wrinkled her nose. "Too red. I liked the other better."

"It's perfect!" Hayley argued. "I want it."

Evie put the shirt back on the rack. "I'm sure glad you guys came to the mall tonight. I thought I was going to have to sit in the Hair House with nothing to do but watch Mom's hair curl."

"Your mom won't let you walk around?" Candace asked.

Evie shook her head. "Not by myself. She says it's too dangerous. She thinks there are too many weirdos around."

"Moms always think that," Candace said, rolling her eyes.

"Hey," Hayley whispered, "look at that guy's boots."

Both Evie and Candace turned. The man walked over to a rack of coats. As he did, little silver spurs on his boots jingled. He smiled at the girls.

Protection from strangers

"You like spurs?" Candace asked. "I don't even like boots."

"Come on. Let's go," Evie said. They wandered through the mall stores, having a soda at the ice-cream shop and watching the game players at the arcade.

When they stopped at the pet shop, they heard a voice down by the exit. "Candace! Candace, come on."

"It's my mom," Candace said. "I guess we have to go, Hayley. See you later, Evie."

" 'Bye." Evie waved and didn't really think about being alone until she turned to walk away. *Mom would have a fit if she knew I was all alone out here. Oh well, what she doesn't know won't worry her. I'll just walk back to the Hair House.*

Evie turned a corner and headed to the escalator. She loved riding up so she could watch the people below get shorter and farther away. As she neared the top, the man with the silver spurs on his boots stepped on at the bottom.

Someone should tell him that the western store is downstairs, Evie thought as she turned away. Then she had an idea. *I'll stop by that bookstore and get a magazine to read while I wait for Mom.* A few steps down the hall to her right brought her to the open doors of . . . The Furniture Shop?

"Hey, where's the bookstore?" Evie asked out loud. No one answered, so she turned and stared up and down the mall. "I know it was here before," she muttered.

Then she remembered. *It's on the other side of Candy-by-the-Ton. By that craft place, I think.* As she turned to go back past the escalator, she saw that the man with the spurs was looking at the furniture.

After a few more turns, Evie found the craft shop. But the bookstore wasn't there. *Where is it? Where am I?* Suddenly, she felt a little nervous. *I'd better find one of those mall maps.*

She heard footsteps behind her and turned to ask if that person knew where the bookstore was. "Do you—" Then she froze. It was the man with the silver spurs. He was smiling at her, but something about that smile made goose bumps come up on her arms.

Without saying another word, Evie turned and ran down the mall away from him. She ducked into the first store she came to.

Dodging past a display of beautiful glass animals, Evie walked quickly down the aisle. *I think that man is following me! What am I going to do? Oh, Candace and Hayley, come back!*

She stopped beside a rack of birthday cards. Rubbing her arms with both hands, she picked a card. But she was too nervous to even see the words. Then she heard a sound that made her almost stop breathing.

Jingle, jingle. The man with the spurs walked in.

He really is following me! What am I going to do?

Without even looking back, Evie ducked down the farthest aisle and walked quickly to the end. There, behind a rack of doll clothes, she tried to think. *What did Mother say I should*

Happy to be Arrested!

do if I'm in danger? Look for a police officer or an adult in charge. But there's no one around except him!

Then she heard it again. The *jingle, jingle* sound was getting closer. She peeked down the aisle. He was coming right toward her!

Just then, a woman in a blue uniform grabbed Evie's shoulder from behind. "Hold it right there," she said. "I'm the security guard here," the woman said, "and I'm going to arrest you for shoplifting."

Evie almost fainted. "But—I didn't—but . . ."

"Where are your parents?" the woman demanded.

"My mom's at . . ." Evie started to answer, but the security officer wasn't even looking at her. "Was that man following you?" she asked quietly.

Evie could only nod her head.

The woman patted her arm. "I thought so. Just a moment." She held up a radio and spoke into it. "Security, this is Pam in Crystal Palace. We have a possible abduction attempt. Male, medium height, wearing boots with silver spurs."

After answering a few questions, she turned back to Evie. "Are you OK?"

Evie nodded. "Where did you come from? I thought I was alone."

"That big mirror at the end is really a security door. I was watching you. Then I popped out and grabbed you."

"I really didn't steal anything," Evie said.

Pam laughed. "Oh, I know that. I just said that to scare him off."

Evie was confused. "What?"

"I was watching you through the security mirrors, and I thought you were scared. But I didn't know if he was the

problem. I figured I'd come out and arrest you for shoplifting.
If he was your dad or something, he'd come right over. If he
wasn't, he'd take off. Just like he did."

Evie started to relax. "Thanks. I've never seen that man before tonight, but he's been following me for a long way."

Pam frowned. "If you're ever caught all alone like that again and someone is scaring you, the best thing to do is scream. As loud as you can. That will get everyone's attention, and the bad person will usually leave."

"I can do that," Evie decided.

"Great. Now, where are your parents?"

Evie's eyes got big. "My mom's down at the Hair House. She's probably having a fit worrying about me."

"Come on," Pam said. "I'll take you there."

"Wait until I tell her how I was arrested for shoplifting," Evie said with a laugh. "She'll be so happy!"

A Skunk by the Tail 5

I dare you!"

Steven looked down at where his cousin Kyle was sitting on a branch. Past Kyle, the ground looked like a million miles away.

"Drop from this high up?" he said. "I dare you to do it."

Kyle looked down. "No way. I dared you first."

Slam! Below them, the back-porch door closed behind the boys' Great-grandfather Steuben. "Vere are those two boys?" A floating leaf made him look up. "Vat! Are you trying to be killed?"

"Hi, Grandpa Steuben," Kyle called. "Steven was about to drop down to the ground."

"I was not!"

Grandpa shook his head. "All boys must be crazy." He looked back up at his grandsons. "If you fall down and break both your legs, don't come running to me! Humf!" He turned and headed around the house to his garden.

Dealing with dares

Steven and Kyle loved the two weeks they spent every summer at their great-grandparents' house. The boys were nearly the same age, and every year, they had to prove again who was the best. Steven could climb faster; Kyle finished their races a half-step ahead. Steven won most games of checkers; Kyle won at dominos.

The porch door opened again. "Boys! Boys? Vell, I guess these cookies vill grow cold and lonely."

Steven looked at Kyle. "Coming, Grandma!" they both shouted as they raced to the ground.

Their cookies had just disappeared when Grandpa stomped in. "All my hard vork in the garden, and a skonk digs it up. Vat I need is a good shotgun."

"Grandpa, control your temper," Grandma scolded. "Ve are teaching these boys to care for nature, not destroy it. The skunk does vhat all skunks do."

Grandpa sighed and nodded. Then a half-smile spread over his face. "You remember Dieter, from the old country?"

Grandma smiled too. "He knew how to fix a skonk problem, eh?"

They both laughed in a quiet, distant way and then shook their heads. Kyle spoke up. "What did Dieter do about the skunk?"

"Vat? Oh, Dieter. He found a way to move a skonk without the spraying and stinking. He says if you pick up a skonk by the tail, it cannot spray you."

"Is that true?" Steven asked.

"Vat? A skonk by the tail? Yes, I guess it is true." Grandpa chuckled again, then closed his eyes.

Later, the boys sat on the stone wall by the garden, resting from a race through the woods. "Hey, what's that?" Kyle

A Skunk by the Tail

asked as he pointed down the wall.

Steven stretched for a better look at the animal walking along the ground. "It's a skunk! It must be headed back to Grandpa's garden."

"I dare you to grab it," Kyle said quietly.

"What? You lost your mind?"

Kyle rolled his eyes. "Grandpa said it was safe to pick up a skunk by the tail. All you have to do is lie here. When the skunk walks by underneath with its tail up—grab it!"

"I dare you to do it," Steven whispered.

"I dared you first," Kyle hissed back. "Are you afraid?"

Steven rolled over and reached toward the ground. Yes, he probably could reach the skunk. *I don't want Kyle to think I'm afraid*, he thought. "OK, I'll do it."

Steven watched the skunk as it wandered along, stopping to scratch and sniff as it went. When it came close, he hardly dared blink. When it was right underneath him, he stopped breathing.

He slowly reached down toward the skunk's back. Then, with a quick grab, he snatched the skunk by the tail and held it up!

"I did it! I got him!"

"You really did it!" Kyle stared with his mouth hanging open. "That's amazing."

The skunk hissed and twisted, but Steven held it tight. "It can't spray as long as I'm holding the tail," he bragged.

Kyle looked at the skunk's angry eyes. "Do you think you're hurting it? Maybe you should put it down."

"If you say so," Steven agreed. He bent over, then quickly straightened up. "Wait a minute. If I set it down, it'll spray me for sure."

Kyle blinked. "But you can't hold it forever. You have to put it down." Suddenly, he started backing away, toward the house.

"Hey, this was your idea," Steven said, trying not to panic. "What am I supposed to do?"

"Just drop it and run as fast as you can," Kyle said from a safe distance.

Steven looked around, but no better ideas showed up.

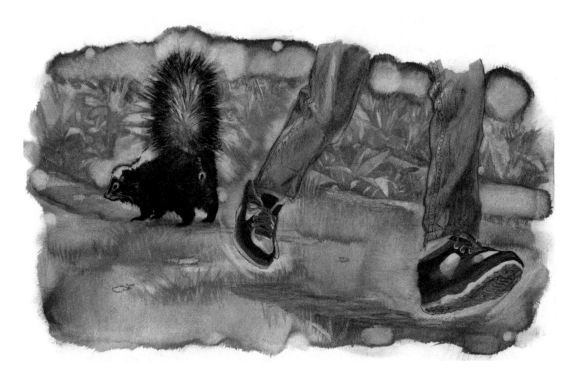

He bent his knees and held the skunk out as far as he could. Then he turned the tail loose and spun, running faster than he had ever run before.

It wasn't fast enough. Steven smelled the skunk spray before he took two steps. Still he ran, catching up with Kyle as they both ran straight for the back-porch door.

A Skunk by the Tail

Grandma was there first. "Vat is that awful . . . boys, you didn't . . ."

"He did," Kyle said as he raced up and stood behind her. "Steven grabbed the skunk."

"It was Kyle's idea," Steven wailed as Grandma covered her nose with her apron. His eyes were burning and stinging now.

"Kyle, go get your grandfather. Then get that old blanket in the garage. Steven, go stand over there by the hose."

Before long, Grandpa arrived. "Vat in the vorld vere you boys thinking?"

"Later, Grandpa," Grandma said. "Steven, take off those smelly clothes. Grandpa, wrap him in the blanket. Then go to the store for some tomato juice. Lots of tomato juice."

Steven moaned again when he sat in the yard wrapped up in the blanket. Kyle tried to slip away to his room.

"Not so fast, Mr. Bright Ideas," Grandma said. "You go get the shovel and bury those clothes in the voods."

"But . . ." The look on Grandma's face stopped Kyle's next

A Skunk by the Tail

words. He went to get the shovel.

Much later, after much tomato juice, they all sat on the porch while Grandma combed Steven's hair. "Vhy vould you grab a skunk?" she asked.

"Kyle dared me to," Steven admitted sheepishly.

"And this meant you had to do it?" she asked. "Vat if he dared you to stand in front of a train? You vould do this?"

"I didn't want him to think I was afraid," Steven said quietly.

"I'm sorry, Steven. I thought it was OK to grab a skunk," Kyle protested. "Grandpa said Dieter did it in the old country."

"Dieter didn't like to think," Grandma said, tapping her head. "He did anything people dared him to do."

"I think maybe ve got the same problem here," Grandpa said in a loud voice.

"Not any more," Steven declared. "I don't care what Kyle or anyone says. I'll do what I think is right, even if they think I'm a chicken."

"Me too," Kyle said.

The Hard Way

We're going to make a ton of money," Daniel bragged as he pedaled. "That old dump is full of aluminum cans, and when we turn them in for recycling, we'll have enough money to last all summer."

"I hope you're right," Jose said as they coasted into Mike's yard on their bikes. "Hey, Mike, you ready to go?"

Mike popped out the door and walked over to them with one hand behind his back. "You guys want to see something?" he asked.

"Sure," Daniel said. "Is it something we're taking to the dump with us?"

"I'd like to," Mike answered. Then he pulled it out.

"Hey, that's a gun," Jose said. "What are you doing with it?"

"A gun!" Daniel echoed. "Cool! Can I see it?"

Mike held it out, one finger on the trigger guard. "It's my dad's pistol," he explained. "He uses it to target shoot—and to

Dealing with guns

kill water moccasins when he goes fishing. Do you like it?" He pointed it toward them as he asked.

"Stop that!" Jose shouted. "Don't you know anything about guns? Stop pointing that thing at us!"

"Oh, stop whining," Mike said. "It's not loaded."

"We're leaving," Jose said quickly. "Come on, Daniel."

Daniel still wanted to look at the gun. "But, Jose, I just wanted to—"

Jose cut him off. "I'm leaving now. Mike, we'll meet you at the dump—without that gun." Then he spun his bike around and took off. After a second of hesitation, Daniel followed him.

"Why didn't you want to look at it, Jose?" he asked as he rode along beside.

"That wasn't a toy," Jose said. "That pistol could kill you."

"But Mike said it wasn't loaded."

Jose shook his head. "My dad says that lots of people get killed every day by guns that aren't loaded. At least, someone thinks they aren't loaded. But when the trigger is pulled, they find out they were wrong—dead wrong."

The dump lived up to its name. Bottles, cans, pieces of old furniture, and stuff were scattered everywhere. "There's an aluminum can," Jose said. "And there's another. You were right about this place."

Before they had many cans, Mike rode up. "So, did you find much?" He was carrying a rifle.

"Hey, I told you—"

Mike held up his hand. "Relax, Jose. This is just my BB gun. I only brought it along for protection. From rats or bees or whatever."

"Wow, a BB gun," Daniel said. He ran over to see it up close. "Can I try a shot or two?"

"Maybe later. If we can find something to shoot at," Mike answered. For a while, the boys kept busy, picking up the scattered aluminum cans and stuffing them in their bags. Then Daniel saw something move. Something big!

"Whoa! What was that?" he shouted, jumping up on an old washing machine. Then he saw it again. "It's a rat!"

"Keep an eye on it," Mike said. He ran over to his bike, grabbed the BB gun, and raced back, cocking the gun as he ran.

"Hey, watch it!" Jose yelled as the gun went right past his face.

"There he goes," Daniel reported. The rat ran. Mike pulled the trigger. *Snap!* The BB bounced off a tin can. Mike cocked

the gun and shot again. *Crack!* The BB broke an old peanut butter jar.

"You missed him," Jose said as the rat disappeared inside a molding couch.

"But look at that jar," Mike said. "It cracked in half. Good shot, huh?"

"Let me try it," Daniel asked.

"Wait. Let's set up several bottles on this box and shoot at them," Mike answered. He began to line up dirty old bottles on the box. Daniel started to help him.

"I'm not so sure that's a good idea," Jose said. "This is not our property. It might not be safe to shoot at glass like that."

"What's wrong with breaking a few bottles?" Mike asked. "Besides, this dump doesn't belong to anyone."

"Well, the BB could bounce back and hit someone. Or a glass could shatter and cut someone," Jose said.

Mike laughed at Jose. "What are you, some kind of chicken? I've done this lots of times." He aimed at the first bottle and fired. *Crack!* The bottle's pieces slid to the ground. "Now, watch me break that big green one."

Pooff! Nothing happened. "I must be out of BBs." Mike shook the gun. There was no rattling sound. "Too bad."

"Aw, I wanted to shoot," Daniel complained. With a sigh, he went back to looking for cans. He found a bunch of them next to a big crate. "Hey, guys, here's a ton of them. Bring another bag." Then he heard a sound that made him spin around.

Buzzzz! "Whoa!" he shouted as he dodged away.

"What is it?" Mike shouted. "Another rat?"

Daniel stopped when he got to where Jose was. "No, it's a wasp—I mean a bunch of them. On a big nest."

"Where?" Mike wanted to see it.

"Right inside that crate," Daniel reported. "See, right in the corner."

Mike picked up his gun and stepped closer. "Boy, if I had more BBs, I'd show those wasps a thing or two." He peered inside the crate. "I could just stand here and pick them off one at a time." He cocked the gun and aimed. "Yeah, I got 'em right in my sights."

He pulled the trigger. *Snap!* A BB shot out. *Crack!* It hit the wasp nest. Wasps went everywhere!

"Yikes!" Mike shouted. "Run!"

Daniel and Jose were already running. But not far. Daniel's foot hit a piece of wire. He hit the ground. "Ooof! Ow!"

Jose tripped over an old bucket. "Whoa!" he shouted as he fell. *Crack!* His hand hit a glass jar.

When they finally made it back to their bikes, Mike had been stung twice, Daniel had a scrape on his arm, and Jose was dripping blood from a cut on his hand. "Come on," Jose said, pressing his hand against his shirt, "my mom's home." They rode slowly and shakily to Jose's house.

Jose's mother teased them. "I don't know who started this war, but I can see who lost. What did the other guys look like?"

"They were this big," Daniel reported, holding his fingers about an inch apart, "red, and they had wings. And they were mad." He thumped Mike's arm. "Thanks to you!"

"Hey, I didn't think I could really hit their nest. I didn't even think the BB gun was loaded!"

After everyone had to been cleaned up and treated, they retired to the front porch to eat Popsicles. "Maybe my dad will help us get our bags of cans when he gets home," Jose said.

Mike stood up. "Well, would you guys get my gun too? I don't really want to go back there today." Jose nodded, and Mike rode away. Slowly.

Daniel shook his head. "I guess you were right about guns that aren't loaded. Look what happened to us—and it was just a BB gun that wasn't loaded!" He sighed. "But I never got to try shooting."

"You can shoot mine sometime," Jose said.

"You have a BB gun?"

Jose nodded. "But I can only shoot it when my dad's around. Let's see if he'll set up some targets for us in the backyard after we get the cans from the dump."

Daniel's face broke into a grin. Then it clouded over. "Do

doesn't get out soon."

Jenny worried and watched the bird all through church. It flew nervously between the lights near the ceiling but never came down near any of the people. After the last hymn, others began walking out, but Jenny stayed in her seat.

"Jenny, are you ready to go? It's time for lunch, you know." Her mother was standing at the door.

"Mom, I'm not hungry. Besides, we can't go. What about the bird? We can't let it die. We have to save it!"

Pastor Romero walked up as Jenny was speaking. "I have an idea, Jenny. Mr. Green and I are going to close all the win-

dows. Will you pull the dark shades down and cover them? Then if your mother will turn off all the lights, we'll open the door again, and maybe the bird will fly out to get to the sunshine."

Jenny jumped up, and in a few minutes, the room was very dark. Then Pastor Romero opened the door, and sunshine streamed in. "Now, let's all sit and be very still. Maybe the bird will see that this is the way out. Maybe it will follow the sun-

shine right out the door."

Jenny sat and watched. She couldn't see the bird in the darkness of the ceiling, but she heard its *cheep, cheep*. She watched the doorway and the band of sunlight that spread across the floor. *Come on, little bird. Follow the sunlight.* Suddenly, a shadow zipped by her head and right out the door.

"There it goes! It's out! We saved it," she shouted. "Oh, Mom, I'm so glad it won't die."

They said goodbye to Pastor Romero and were on their way to the car, when Jenny stopped. "Now I understand," she said.

"Understand what, Jenny?"

"What you said yesterday about Jesus. About Him being the only One who can save us from sin."

"What?"

"It's like that bird. It flew around, up there in the lights, lost and confused. But when it saw the light from the door, it followed the sunshine and was saved. We're stuck, too, in our world where people get hurt and everything dies. But Jesus knows the only way out. If we follow Him, He'll save us from our sin and selfishness."

Jenny found her mother's arms wrapped around her again. "That's right, Jenny, and soon He'll take us to a place where nothing gets old and no one ever dies. Oh, Jenny, I'm so glad you know Jesus."

"Me too, Mom. Now take me home. I'm starving!"

Follow the Sunlight

Beautiful and Mysterious

13

Did you get them?"

Sonia's voice hissed like a leaking bicycle tire. She raced down the alleyway after Alyssa.

Alyssa finally stopped behind a big dumpster. "Here," she said, pulling two slightly mangled cigarettes out of her pocket. "I don't think anyone saw me."

Sonia took one and smoothed it out straight. "How do I look?" she asked, putting the cigarette between her lips. "Do I look beautiful and mysterious, like the woman in that magazine?"

"No," Alyssa answered. "The magazine woman is holding her cigarette like this." She raised her arm and dangled her cigarette between two fingers. "It's very glamorous."

Slam!

Both girls jumped like they had been shot. Sonia grabbed Alyssa's arm. "What was that?" she whispered.

"It sounded like the back door of my house," Alyssa said.

Dealing with smoking

"Come on. Let's go."

Sonia held out her cigarette. "Here, you keep this."

"No way," Alyssa said. She threw both cigarettes into the dumpster and led the way back toward her house. "Look, my Uncle Tim's on the back porch smoking."

Sonia clutched Alyssa's arm. "You don't think he knows you took those cigarettes, do you?"

"Ow! Stop strangling my arm. No, I took them out of an old pack he threw in the trash. Come on. Let's go talk to him."

The girls walked up to the porch. "Good evening, girls," Tim said. "What are you up to this time?"

Sonia gasped. Alyssa punched her arm and said, "Not much. Just wandering around the neighborhood." She watched him flick ashes onto the grass.

Tim nodded. "I'm just out catching a smoke, myself. You know your mother won't let me smoke in the house."

"Why do you smoke, Uncle Tim?" Alyssa asked. She watched his face carefully.

He took another puff. "I guess it relaxes me, kind of calms me down." He chuckled and pulled the pack out of his shirt pocket. "It's funny to be calmed by something that says it could kill you right on the package."

Alyssa had read the warning about lung cancer and emphysema.

Uncle Tim laughed again. "But you never think it'll happen to you. And so far, so good." He tossed the butt into a trash can and headed back in. "I'd better be headed home. See you girls later."

"I have to go in too," Alyssa said to Sonia. "I'll see you tomorrow."

In her room, Alyssa opened the magazine with the picture and laid it on her bed. The woman's beautiful face, perfect smile, and elegant fingernails shone out from the page. Between her fingers was a long white cigarette. The words said *She's beautiful and mysterious—the Elegance Cigarette woman.*

Alyssa picked up a pencil and held it between her fingers. "Why, yes, I'd love to," she said in a deep, soft voice.

"You'd love to what?" The voice crashed in on Alyssa's imagination. She dropped the pencil and fell back onto the bed.

"Mom! You scared me to death!"

"Sorry," her mother said. "Who were you talking to, anyway?"

Alyssa leaned across the open magazine. "I was talking to myself."

Her mother's eyebrows went up. "I see. Well, supper's ready. Come and eat."

After supper, Alyssa read another magazine while her dad watched TV. She looked up when a commercial showed a beautiful woman with a perfect smile. "New Perfect-White tooth cleaner will make your smile shine. Just apply for thirty minutes once a month."

"That sounded easier than brushing your teeth every day," she said out loud.

Her mother snorted. "As long as you want perfect white teeth with holes in them."

The woman on the commercial added, "It even works on smokers' teeth!"

"Do smokers have dirty teeth?" Alyssa asked.

"Have you ever looked at your Uncle Tim's teeth?" Dad asked. "They're as yellow as a beaver's. That's what the smoke does to them if you smoke long enough."

"And to your fingers too," her mom added. She held up two fingers. "Most smokers have yellow stains on the fingers they hold their cigarettes with."

"Ugh," Alyssa said. *There must be a way to keep that from happening*, she thought. *After all, that model in the magazine has beautiful teeth and fingers.*

The next morning, Sonia called. "Alyssa, it's too hot to just sit around the house. Let's go to the pool."

"Wait a second. I'll ask my mom." She put her hand over the phone. "Mom! Can I go to the pool with Sonia?"

"I don't have time to take you," Mom called back.

Alyssa thought for a second. "I could take the bus. It goes right to the city park."

"OK," Mom answered. "But you have to be back by three."

Before long, Alyssa was sitting on a city bus next to someone's grandmother. She pulled the magazine out of her back-

pack and turned to the model with the cigarette. *I could be beautiful and mysterious,* she said to herself.

Holding two fingers up to her lips, Alyssa pretended to puff on a cigarette.

"She looks glamorous, doesn't she?" a voice croaked in her ear.

"Ah!" Alyssa jerked away. It was the grandmother. "I'm sorry. You scared me."

"I do sound strange, don't I?" the woman said. "I saw you looking at the model. I used to be a model." She croaked a laugh at the look on Alyssa's face. "It was a long time ago. But I used to model clothes. And cigarettes, like that woman."

"What happened to your voice?" Alyssa asked.

The woman pulled back a scarf to show a shiny metal circle on her throat. "I have to breathe through this thing," she explained. "When I got throat cancer, the doctors had to take out my voice box."

Alyssa's hand went up to her own throat.

"You see," the woman went on, "I didn't just model for cigarette companies. I smoked the cigarettes too. And this is what happened. It's really glamorous, don't you think?"

Alyssa found Sonia in the pool changing room. "Look," Sonia said. She reached into her pack. "I found a cigarette in the laundromat." She held one up to her lips. "Do I look mysterious and alluring?"

Alyssa slapped it out of her hand. "You look stupid. Don't ever smoke one of those!"

Sonia's eyes got really big.

Alyssa laughed. "Let me explain."

Great Stories for Kids

Your children will love the adventures and drama of the five-volume set *Great Stories for Kids*, and you'll value the character-building lessons they learn while reading these treasured stories. Each volume is bound in durable hardcover with delightful color illustrations. Also available in Spanish and French.

The Bible Story

The Bible Story was written not just to tell the wonderful stories in the Bible, but each story was especially written to teach your child a different character-building lesson—lessons such as honesty, respect for parents, obedience, kindness, and many more. This is truly the pleasant way to influence your child's character. The set contains more than 400 stories spread over 10 volumes. Hardcover.

Uncle Arthur's Bedtime Stories

For years this collection of stories has been the center of cozy reading experiences between parents and children. Arthur Maxwell tells the real-life adventures of young children—adventures that teach the importance of character traits such as kindness and honesty. Five volumes, hardcover.

Quigley's Village (video series for kids)

Quigley's videos, for ages 2-7, teach children biblical values through the adventures of Mr. Quigley and his lovable puppet friends. They are filled with stories, songs, humor, and fun, helping children to learn and grow. Perfect for teaching values at home, school, or church. They are approximately 30 minutes in length.

For more information, mail the postpaid card, or write to:
Pacific Press® Marketing Service, P.O. Box 5353. Nampa, ID 83683

Yes, please send me information on the following:

- ❏ **GREAT STORIES FOR KIDS**
- ❏ **THE BIBLE STORY**
- ❏ **UNCLE ARTHUR'S BEDTIME STORIES**
- ❏ **QUIGLEY'S VILLAGE**

Name_____

Address_____

City_____

State_____Zip_____

Phone (_____)_____

Yes, please send me information on the following:

- ❏ **GREAT STORIES FOR KIDS**
- ❏ **THE BIBLE STORY**
- ❏ **UNCLE ARTHUR'S BEDTIME STORIES**
- ❏ **QUIGLEY'S VILLAGE**

Name_____

Address_____

City_____

State_____Zip_____

Phone (_____)_____

BUSINESS REPLY MAIL

FIRST-CLASS MAIL PERMIT NO. 300 NAMPA ID

POSTAGE WILL BE PAID BY ADDRESSEE

PACIFIC PRESS® PUBLISHING ASSOCIATION
MARKETING SERVICE
PO BOX 5353
NAMPA ID 83653-9903

BUSINESS REPLY MAIL

FIRST-CLASS MAIL PERMIT NO. 300 NAMPA ID

POSTAGE WILL BE PAID BY ADDRESSEE

PACIFIC PRESS® PUBLISHING ASSOCIATION
MARKETING SERVICE
PO BOX 5353
NAMPA ID 83653-9903